For my mother, my angel.
Thank you for lighting this path of mine.
I love you.

For my dear editor, Karen Austin (AKA "Hollywood").
Thank you for your friendship, your wisdom, and genuineness.
You encouraged me to grow and pushed me to strive for better.
I'm forever grateful.

This book is dedicated to anyone who has ever lost
someone they loved dearly. May you take comfort in knowing that
they are with us, still.

With love and gratitude,
Heather

This book is given with love

To

_____

From

_____

Author: Heather Lean

Developmental Editor: Karen Austin

Illustrators: Sudipta Dasgupta and Nina Aptsiauri

To see more of our books, visit us at:
www.PuppyDogsAndIceCream.com

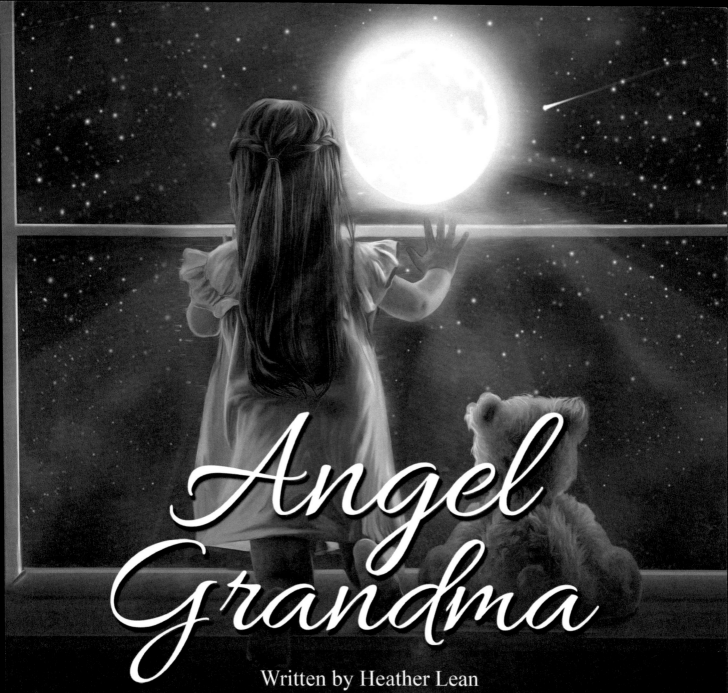

Angel Grandma

Written by Heather Lean

As the Sun begins to rise

In the dewy morning air,

I am your Angel Grandma

My love is always there.

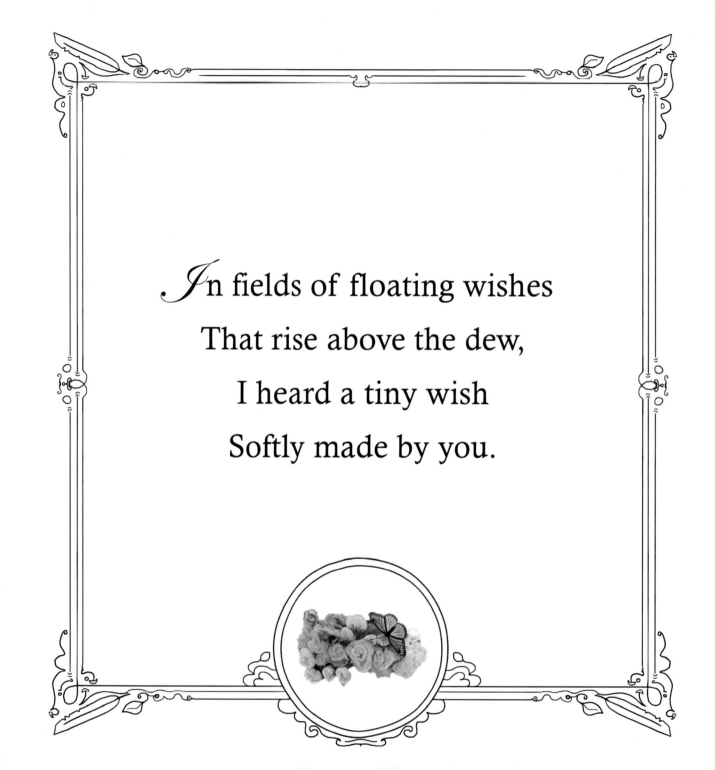

*I*n fields of floating wishes

That rise above the dew,

I heard a tiny wish

Softly made by you.

While swinging in the breeze
Your spirit shines so bright,
The laughter that I hear
Is ringing with delight.

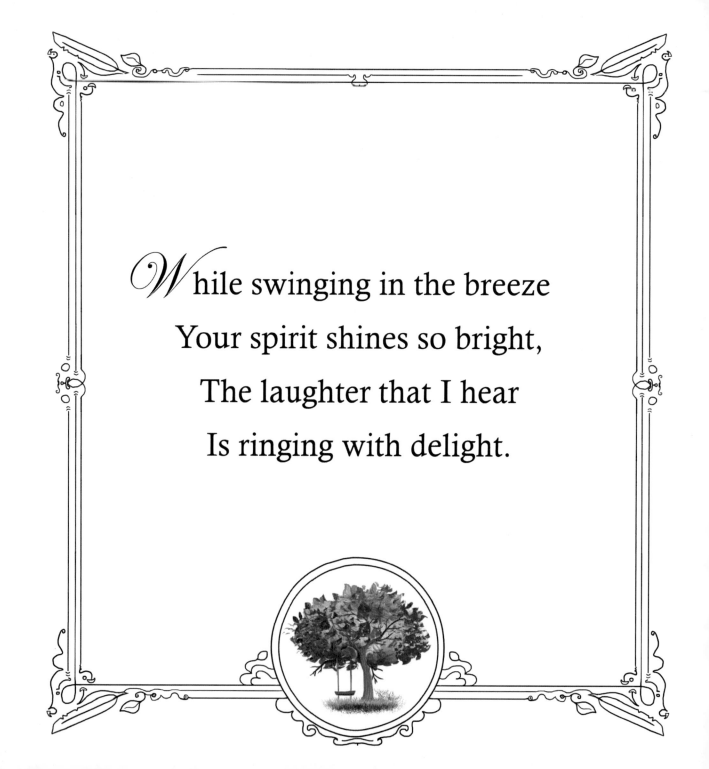

The music that you make
While playing your sweet song,
Will find a way to me
So I can hum along.

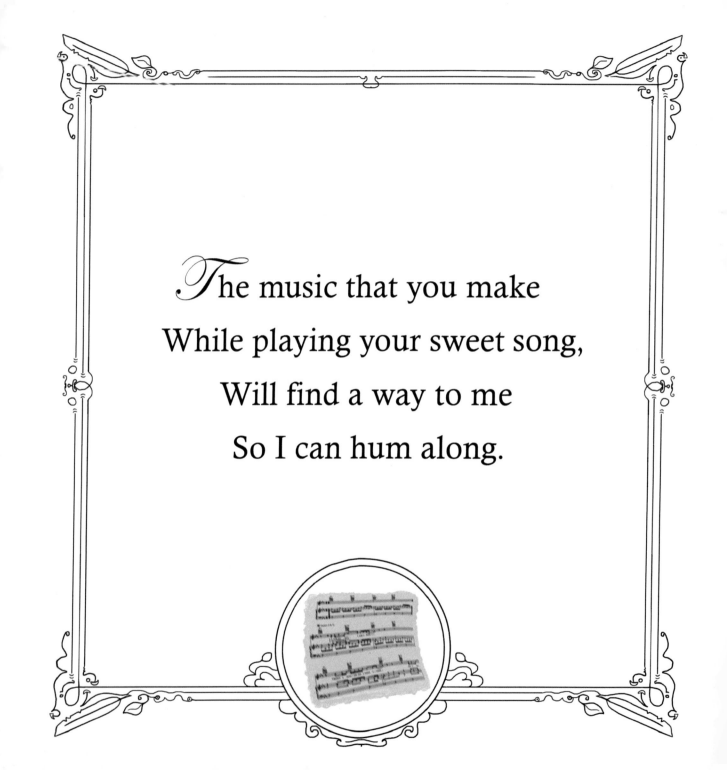

Your friends among the trees

Can feel my presence too,

The creatures know my spirit

Is watching over you.

When riding on your bike

Wherever you may roam,

My love is with you always

Even far from home.

$\mathcal{A}$ treasure in the sand

Can help you to remember,

The special times we shared

When we were together.

$\mathcal{I}$ am with you always
Although not in plain sight,
My love glows within you
Like fireflies at night.

And when the evening comes

Look up to find my star,

I will always be there

No matter where you are.

It's time to tuck you in

So snuggle up and sleep,

I'll be waiting for you

To find me in your dreams.

And so my darling grandchild
As sure as stars will shine,
My heart lives on within you
Until the end of time.

I Love You

Write a Memory

Write a message or special moment below
to remember your Angel Grandma by.

_____

_____

_____

_____

_____

_____

Capturing Moments

Include a photo of your grandma here.

About the Author

Heather Lean is an attorney and a mom of two. Her first book, Angel Grandma, was written after grieving the loss of her mother-in-law and her mother.

After writing this book, she found herself writing several others, and it was the spark that ignited her passion for writing children's books. All of Heather's books have a central theme of Love.

Heather resides in New York, where she enjoys spending time with her family, friends, and pets. She has four hens, three cats, and a puppy named Beau.

Other Books by the Author:

Angel Grandpa

Climbing that old oak tree
Laughing in its shade,
Searching for the squirrels
As they gathered nuts and played.

🐾 Claim Your FREE Gift!

Visit 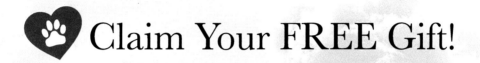 <u>PDICBooks.com/gift</u>

Thank you for purchasing Angel Grandma, and
welcome to the Puppy Dogs & Ice Cream family.

We're certain you're going to love the little gift
we've prepared for you at the website above.

Made in the USA
Middletown, DE
02 March 2021